Editor: Konstantinos Fylatos
Author: CHRISTOPHER BALIS

Artwork by Manolis Frangidis

© Fylatos Publishing
e-mail: contact@fylatos.com
web: www.fylatos.com

ISBN: 978-960-658-353-7

LITTLE DROPS OF HORROR

Memoirs of Monsters

By: Christopher Balis

Fylatos Publishing
MMXXV

ACKNOWLEDGMENTS

This book, as much as any other book, did not write itself. Aside from the tenuous efforts of the author, there are others who played a vital part in making this book a reality.

I would therefore like to thank my family, for teaching me to see the world with inquiring eyes.

I send out my deepest gratitude to my Alpha and Beta readers, who courageously delved into rough drafts, and provided me with their honest opinions and recommendations: Annie Lee, Cyril Mullins, Apostolos Smoloktos, Chrysa Pantazi, Dimitris Karagkanis, Dimitris Kolovos, Philippos Antoniadis, Thanasis Kostopoulos, Panos Rigopoulos.

At this point, I also thank my other dear friends from the bottom of my heart, who believed in me and my dream when I most needed it: Alexandros Kartsonis, Alexandros Tiliakos, Eirini Kokolaki, Manos Gallios, Maria Kyrlagitsi, Sakis Binopoulos, Stelios Tzanis.

For all that and even more,

Thank you.

CONTENTS

vi

DIARY OF A FLESH EATER

At nights I prey upon the living and the dead, forever haunted by my relentless stalker. Cursed with a never-ending hunger for human flesh, succulent marrow, and bone, albeit blessed with life everlasting, or at least, a vile imitation of it.

The embrace of darkness finds me driven to scribble these notes for reasons unknown to me, in this dank and abandoned subway station, in hopes of someone stumbling upon them. Perhaps it is the vanity of a cursed existence to make its presence known and in that way find peace. But it feels like something deeper. I am certain that my compulsion to write this account of my life cannot be attributed to the triviality of dining on an ex-college professor this fine night. Mind you, my tendency to consume human flesh comes not out of some sickened sense of enjoyment; even though I must admit that after all these years I can find a certain pleasure in it. With no other option, if I were to suffer every time I gain sustenance, it would make my semblance of a life a living hell.

These are not the ramblings of a madman[1].

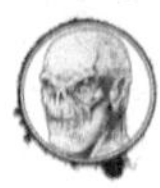

My name is Fazul[2] Hazem, and I was born in the region of the world currently known as Libya, on the day that the Ottoman Empire conquered Constantinople[3]. My parents always said that because of that, I was destined to become a great man. Allah be praised that they have long passed, and they cannot witness my current state. I spent most of my human life herding goats, and sometimes escorting travellers across the desert. The latter was a difficult and dangerous occupation, albeit a profitable one. It was upon my return from one of those journeys that my fate changed forever, when I stumbled upon those accursed ruins.

I still remember the merciless sun of that day, and how I prayed for respite. The scorching sands beneath my sandals scalded my toes and made my feet blister. As if to mock any answer to my prayers, a warm Southern Wind[4] began to flow over the dunes foretelling the coming of a sandstorm. I laughed at my misfortune and guided my camels onward in search of shelter, but none had been found by the time the storm fell upon us. One of my camels broke away in fear, but the other remained crouching by my side. After the howling wind ceased, I was surprised to notice that a stone structure had been uncovered beneath the sand. The camel that remained stopped several pik away and would not budge, despite my commands with words or use of the lash. I grabbed my spear and proceeded alone.

You must excuse my use of metrics from older times; one pik equates to two-thirds of a metre. I will try to refrain from such habits from now on.

With closer inspection, I realised the structure was quite large, perhaps an entire building or temple from centuries long past. The stonework looked ancient, with a parched, porous texture to it, and was topped with a high pointed tip. I scooped away some of the sand with my bare hands and engravings, much faded by the sands of time, appeared on the surface. For a poor goat herder such as myself reading was seldom, if ever, needed, but it was clear that the text was not in Arabic. If I had trusted the wisdom of my beast of burden at that moment, I might have gone on to live a normal life. Instead, the misguided perception of finding treasure hidden beneath the sands, revealed to me by the Southern Wind, prompted me to proceed and dig up the rest like a fool.

I worked a day and a night to uncover the entrance to a structure which was several metres tall and a few metres wide. The architecture resembled nothing I had encountered and it was not the work of our great leaders, the Hafsids[5]. This was much older. What seemed at first to be a small pyramid was just the roof of the structure, and its large base was in the shape of a stone cube. Around its exterior surface were carvings of unfamiliar letters and strange pictograms, while its grim entrance stood blocked by a heavy limestone slab. Tired from the exertion of uncovering the structure, I decided to rest before trying to find a way in.

My dreams were filled with riches and splendour that night. I drank fine wine from golden goblets and wore robes of silk adorned with jewels of ruby and sapphire, while a beautiful harem indulged my every desire. It was a sight to behold, if just in my imagination, for what came next resembled a living nightmare. When I tried to open the door the following night with my hand shovel and any other tool I had left, I was greeted with the distant yipping of hyenas[6]. My thoughts were that the predators had smelled my fire and approached in search of food, yet little did I know that they had not come for me...

Certain an attack would come, I secured my remaining camel and stood fast with my spear in hand. I remained there for a time, yet the beasts did not come any closer. They stood instead at a distance and watched me under the moonlit sky. After I was certain that they would not attack, with caution I continued my efforts to enter into the mysterious structure. Hours passed and my hands bled while working the shovel, before a small crack appeared on the limestone slab. The crack expanded and branched out like a vine of decay, until the stone shattered in a cloud of dust. The hyenas howled behind me as if in celebration, but still did not approach.

After the dust had settled, I lit a torch and proceeded into the dark, desolate building. The smell of old death lingered within. In the entrance lay a rusted curved sword, with a handguard of copper in the semblance of a falcon. The small chamber had several masterfully sculpted statues along the walls with precious gems adorning their eyes. They stood in silent vigil over the engraved sarcophagus in the centre. To my surprise, the lid had already been opened, revealing jewels and gold in abandon. I thanked Allah for my good fortune then as I stuffed my pouch with riches. I did not stop for a minute to think about how the sarcophagus had been opened from the inside.

When my pouch was full, I picked up the fallen sword, as I thought that it might fetch a good price in the city. Unbeknownst to me at the time, that impulsive action was the sole thing that would save me from a horrible end. As I exited, I was already dreaming about what I would do with my newfound wealth. Imagine my surprise when I saw a black giant of a man devouring my slain camel. Crouched over a river of blood that stained the sand, the giant feasted on the dismembered body of the poor beast with sickening, crunching noises. The silver moonlight shone from above upon that gruesome spectacle and engraved the scene into my brain, where it has remained ever since.

His naked ebony skin was covered with patches of thick pale fur, while a rich mane flowed free on his shoulders. His long limbs were corded with muscles which at first seemed dry, but within moments I witnessed them bulge and expand to a vigorous size as the giant devoured parts of the slain animal. The creature then turned toward me, as if smelling the cold dread that swept over me in violent surges. He moved without a sound despite his bulk. His facial features were canine, but with a distinct humanoid appearance. His milky white eyes stared into my frozen soul, as the fanged snout took on the semblance of a smirk that exhibited malevolent cunning.

I gasped in horror and took a few steps back with a call to Allah, my pouch of treasure abandoned from my limp grasp onto the bloodstained sand. Still holding the leg he was gnawing on, the giant stood upright, taller than any man. With gore and blood dripping from his maw, he pointed at me and spake. I can still hear the cracking, grating sound that was his voice as I write these words.

"You have assisted me and for that, a debt of gratitude is owed. I was entombed in that despicable prison for a very long time, and you have set me free. They call me Sa'dan the Ghoul[7], the Eater of Men, and you will not find God here. Now I can roam the world again, feasting on the living once more like the sheep that they are, for centuries to come. All that I ask, is that you abandon the treasures you pilfered along with that accursed blade, and you may go in peace. Your life will be spared."

In my blatant ignorance of the Hadith[8], I knew not the devil I faced, nor how to dispose of him[9]. My survival instincts and my greed had gotten the better of me, and convinced me to try the unthinkable. I let the sword fall to the ground and pretended to back away in submission, but after reaching my trusty spear I picked it up and thrust it straight into the monster's side. The giant did not howl in agony as I expected; he did not even flinch. Disdaining to remove my spear from his side, he stepped toward me with murderous intent. Taloned hands stretched out to rip my face off, as I dislodged the spear with a frantic tug and took a few steps back toward the tomb. In my haste, my heel stumbled on the fallen sword and almost cost me my balance, just as the black giant sprang in for the kill. I had just managed to steady my spear's end on the ground, and I aimed the tip at the creature's neck.

A forceful blow threw me a few metres into the chamber and sent me sprawling unconscious on the cold stone floor. When I awoke, Sa'dan the Ghoul was impaled on my spear, and struggled to stand up. The spear's edge had penetrated his lower jaw and came out through the top of his head, with not a drop of blood shed. Yet it appeared he had suffered a grievous wound and his strength ebbed away with each passing moment. My right arm gushed blood, in tatters from the blow of the relentless claws. Without a second thought, I picked up the rusty sword in my good hand and raised it high to take the monster's head clean off.

Sa'dan the Eater of Men looked at me then and said, "Your end is as inevitable as it was for those who failed to strike me down in one blow. But not yet. You will live to regret your actions for as long as I desire. Your existence shall be ruled by fear of me and what I will do to you when I catch you. Time does not matter. Be it centuries, years, months, or days, I will always find you wherever you go. Now strike, and seal your fate."

I did, and the sword struck true.

One would have thought that my story would end there, yet it did not. First came my surprise at the fact that the bleeding from my mangled arm halted when I sat down, and I felt no pain as I drifted into a deep sleep. I felt my heartbeat fade until it stopped altogether. I did not go to Jannah[10] or Jahannam as I had been taught to expect, but to a vast darkness that encompassed everything in a silent, cold stillness. In the utter absence of emotion or sense, I felt the fire of an immeasurable hunger that pulled me back, and called me to action to satiate it, demanding it. A hunger complete and absolute, that left no room for doubt or hesitation.

My senses returned to reveal the butchered body of the camel pulsing red against the night, like a beacon of lifeblood. At first, I was filled with doubt, but after the first bite of that sinewy red meat, I did not stop until the entire animal was devoured. My teeth fell away while I ate, and new, larger ones sprouted in their place which allowed me to chew through bone like butter. My fingers grew talons that could rend and maim, similar to those of the black giant but far smaller. My jaw elongated and stretched, allowing for larger bites.

When I was done with my gruesome meal, I felt my talons retract and my mouth return to its original size. Strength and vigour filled me, and a flood of energy coursed through my body. Before my very eyes, I witnessed my destroyed arm healing with great haste. Its flesh sewed back together and formed a new limb. Under that moonlit desert night sky, with the Southern Wind that carried the cackling laughter of the hyenas in the distance, I was born anew.

With my newfound fortune, I returned to my family and carved out a new life of splendour and opulence for myself. Living as a prince of the sands for seven years, I indulged in every mortal pleasure while I made sure to satisfy my ever hunger. It was enjoyable, to say the least. With my vast resources, the obtaining of humans to feast upon in secrecy while I maintained my public image as a wealthy landowner was a simple matter. During that time, I lived in constant bliss and I often wondered if I was in heaven. Nevertheless, exactly seven years after that terrifying night in the desert, Sa'dan the Ghoul found me and destroyed my happiness forever.

He descended like a whirlwind of death and destruction upon my estate, slayed my armed guards one by one, and wrought havoc on my family. I still remember my wives' screams, as he dismembered them and painted curses on the walls with their blood. He devoured my sons and daughters and laid waste to my parents, their desperate pleas for help a knife in my blackened heart. As I heard my loved ones perish in excruciating agony behind the locked door of my chambers, I knew I had lost everything. Only then did I realise the true meaning of the dark giant's words on that fateful night. Carrying with me nothing but the sword I had used to decapitate my creator and the few jewels I was wearing on my person at the time, I fled through the window of my estate leaving everything behind.

I roamed the world in search of answers and feasted on those I could without raising suspicion. When living humans were not available, I visited graveyards and ate the dead. Dead flesh still satiated my unyielding hunger, but people whose blood still pumped through their veins were much tastier. The younger the better. I did not discriminate on whom I preyed upon, and chose to act like a natural disaster or a plague would. I never stayed in one place for too long, nor did I try to start a new life for myself, fearing that Sa'dan would find me and repeat the circle of destruction all over again. In all that time my search for answers proved fruitless. Seven years later, even after I had made sure to keep out of sight in an almost abandoned graveyard in Egypt where I posed as a gravedigger, he still found me.

With no way to defeat him, I chose to flee once more, this time to a different continent. I must admit that in doing so, I had a faint hope that my grim pursuer would lose track of me for good. How foolish of me to think so, as sure enough, right on time down to the damned minute, the black giant came again in a storm of vengeance to end my existence. I managed to escape after I had suffered severe injuries and fled like a hunted rabbit. This unending pursuit continued for seven and seventy years, like clockwork. By that time, I had found the information I sought within dusty old tomes, but instead of providing me with a glimmer of hope, they pushed me further into despair. According to legend, since I had not managed to slay Sa'dan in one strike when we first met, I was doomed to a bitter end, no matter my efforts to escape it.

Despite all signs to the contrary and against all odds, a plan to imprison him started to formulate in my mind but was interrupted, as this time, the black giant came not in seven years, but in seven months. I had no other option than to flee again. I spread death wherever I went, all the while stalked by my own death in return. Too little time could be found now to make any appropriate preparations to face Sa'dan the Ghoul. My existence turned into a hopeless repetition that came to a full circle, seven and seventy months later. Ever since, my pursuer visits me every seven days, barely leaving me with enough time to think, other than finding sustenance among the human herd.

I have spent centuries in this accursed state, and the search for a way out still tortures me. I do not want to forego this new life I have been brought into, nor its dark gifts, yet I find myself wishing that someday I will find the courage to face my doom-bringer. I know not when this day will come, nor if it will arrive at all. For the moment,

I continue to roam the human world in search of prey, and feast on those unfortunate enough to cross my path.

Perhaps that is the reason I am scribbling these words tonight, as the break of dawn will soon bring Sa'dan the Ghoul to my doorstep in this decrepit station[11], in the underbelly of Detroit. Perhaps my intention is to warn you of the horrors that lurk in the dark places of this world; even though for you to have found my writings can only mean that you live on the fringe of society already. As for this accursed sword of mine with the falcon hilt, I have decided to leave it here along with my writings. May it serve you better than it did me. In any case, and for what it is worth, I pray to Allah that you never meet me nor the devil that stalks me, for it shall be the last meeting you will ever have.

END

THE THREE SPELLS

My life was stolen, and I was condemned to this wretched existence. It was not taken by brigands in the night, but by my own master's hand. Yet, I bear him no grudge, for he was once a great man. My own name does not matter, as I was granted a chance at life only by the same hand that chose to end it. Looking back, for me to have got a glimpse into things most believe impossible during my short time with him was a privilege. In my now diminished state, some solace is found only in the ponder of the events that transpired.

It all began when the Grand Magus Alathaun bought me, as he needed an apprentice to pass on his wisdom after his death. I could not believe my luck, not only was I spared a poor future working the land, like my father had until his hands bled, but I was given a chance to become something more. My existence had not seen nine winters when he took me in, and that memory is clear because my master had asked my father about it during their bargaining. For reasons unknown to me at the time, he had also asked several times if my father was sure that I was born on a Midsummer[12] day. Only when he was satisfied did the exchange take place and my new life begin.

The first few years I spent in the tower were harsh, yet in no way worse than what I had known so far. We lived there alone, as my master claimed that the Art requires solitude and quiet to be studied. Burdened with menial tasks, completing them to my utmost ability every single day meant that my knees bled from scrubbing the cold stone floors. My hands blistered from shovelling the mounds of manure from the stables. Despite my daily toil, the knowledge of reading and writing under the old sage's tutelage was bestowed upon me. His firm hand, accompanied by his relaxed manner, made me feel at ease and helped me become a dedicated student.

Within a short while, I was able to read one of the books from the tower's extensive library that detailed the wonders of nature. This was not an easy task, as the complexity of the information was initially far beyond my youthful mind to comprehend, and it took me the better part of a year to complete reading it. The moment the book was finished, the value and beauty of knowledge that my master had blessed me with struck me. It left me humbled and craving for more. It was then that a silent oath[14] to always serve this great man to whom I owed so much was born. There, behind the window overlooking the village under the pale moon, I took a blade to my palm and let my crimson blood drip onto the rose bushes dozens of feet below, once, twice, thrice[15]. It was Midsummer.

Perhaps it was that impulsive act which condemned me to be neither living nor dead, cursed to linger in this place forevermore. Yet it matters not, for it is what it is. I do not fully understand what has been done to me, but there is no man still walking the earth who can help me. All those who practised the true Art[13] like the magus Al-athaun have perished long ago. Those few who now exist possess but mere grains from the titanic basalt monument that is the Art. But I digress. It saddens me that after hundreds of years my mind, or what is left of it, struggles to maintain a coherent sequence of events over a long period of time. But take care! I do not claim that the accuracy of my recollections is in any way affected by my fuddled thoughts. For this story needs to be told.

My master was renowned for his skill in the Art throughout many kingdoms, and nobles would frequently visit him with requests for a spell, hex, or potion. Even a few kings and queens, whose names shall not be mentioned, paid him a visit. Of course, all of them rewarded him handsomely for his services, which made him a very wealthy man. But the Grand Magus was not interested in gold, other than as a component in alchemical workings, nor was he inclined to "suffer the ignorant nobles for a moment longer than required," as he used to say.

Alathaun valued knowledge above everything else. He referred to almost everyone else but himself, and some scholars, whom he often quoted, as 'ignorants', and for good reason. He would spend most of his time in study of the thick leather-bound tomes and ancient parchments that populated his two private libraries. The magical texts were filled with runes and symbols, in strange languages long ago swept into oblivion by aeons past. He used to claim that it was those books that granted him his skill, yet I think he was only being modest. The way he devoured information was astonishing, as was his ability to recall events that happened many years ago in every detail, despite his advanced age.

During the time he did not spend studying, he would sometimes visit the spell chamber to work on a commission by one noble or another, but otherwise he avoided it. He always claimed that the Art should only be used for one's self when one was in dire need, and even then, frugally. I got the chance to witness him using the Art only when I grew older, and my initiation was completed. It was a mere evocation of a lesser elemental spirit, which he bound to a noble lady's fan. When outstretched and in use, the fan would produce a gentle breeze on the user's face. To my yet 'ignorant' eyes, the spectacle was extraordinary, even if the Grand Magus treated it as if it was child's play. He even giggled while testing the fan, clearly enjoying the results.

There was a gentle side to my master which surfaced every so often. It was evident when he taught me to become literate, as it was when we gifted our fattest pig to the village every year during the tough winter months. That side of his was seen by all, and the villagers were always accepting of him despite their fearful respect. When visitors would ask them for the reason they stayed next to a Magus, the villagers would claim that my master's power protected them from harm. That was true, to an extent.

Alathaun had indeed cast a protective invocation from the top of his stone tower that covered the surrounding area for miles. I know, because I was there when he had to renew the invocation to maintain the effect. The memory seems like yesterday. It was the most beautiful spectacle I had ever seen. Perched there on the roof, the Great Sage uttered unknown words and took a candle flame to a coil of silver strands. The coil caught on fire which did not burn and changed colour into a silvery-white. The candle melted away as if under unbearable heat and, as it did so, the burning coil extended toward the sky. A scintillating web of hair-thin strands sprouted from the Magus's palm in every direction as far as the eye could see, bathing the night in white-hot light. It lasted only a few moments before the silvery flames went out, but it was enough for me to understand the magnitude of my master's skill. I was later informed that this particular invocation would protect the tower and a few miles of the surrounding area from any otherworldly influences.

Despite working wonders, the Grand Magus somehow still always found time for a walk with me in the village and the small pond nearby. When weather permitted we would take our lunch there under the sunlight, and discuss the mysteries of the universe. My master would sit next to his favourite rock, dip his scrawny feet in the water and smoke his thin wooden pipe in abandon. It was one of his favourite pastimes when youths and children from the village played around in the pond, and he could sit there for hours and look at them.

It was not the gaze of a deprived old man with sick desires, but one of someone reliving blissful, carefree memories. It was the side of him that I miss the most. This memory stands out in my mind because something changed in my master's eyes after he acquired that blasted tome for which he had searched so long, for it marked his downfall.

A shady scoundrel who reeked of blood, and worse, delivered it during the night. Alathaun gave the wretched man his payment in a heavy pouch of gold and was granted a large box, which I was tasked to carry inside. It was not heavy, but the wooden container smelled like something was dead inside it. For me to see the book was prohibited, as the Magus deemed it extremely dangerous, and his instructions were to deposit the box in his private library.

It was much later that I gazed upon the horrific details engraved on the dark grimoire's[16] metallic cover. The nameless creatures depicted there, in semblances of half-beasts and other, slithering alien forms, came from an age before man had discovered fire.

I did not see my master again for a fortnight. He remained locked in his chambers for the entire time. He summoned me only to bring him food and change his chamber pots. When he emerged he was different, with a glint in his eye which was not present before. His countenance was chalky white, while the black circles beneath his eyes and his stained garments told of many sleepless and bathless nights. His demeanour had also changed, if only slightly at the time, into one of dour contemplation and strict authority.

Our walks to the pond lessened until they stopped altogether, as day by day it became evident that the Grand Magus now suffered whenever he witnessed the youths playing in the water. It seemed as if their carefree vigour, fresh from the fountain of youth, was an unforgiving lash on my master's soul. I failed to realise then the profound depth of Alathaun's desires.

The situation continued and only worsened with time. My master now lived permanently in his study and summoned me to his side ever so sparingly to teach me this or that. He claimed he considered it time off from his own studies and took pleasure in doing it, yet, despite his words, I could see him glance at the ironbound tome on his desk at every chance he got. After a point, he even granted me permission to use the spell chamber for minor magical workings, and complete access to any of my master's books, except the dark grimoire. Under normal circumstances, I would be overjoyed with my master's generosity, yet I could not help but think it was but a ruse to keep me occupied.

Months passed and then years, before my master unexpectedly announced that he would be using the spell chamber for himself, making it a point that he wanted his privacy. He even went as far as to give me some gold and send me off to the village for the night, instructing me to return on the morrow. That was the first time that I doubted my tutor's intent. His eagerness to dispose of me was disturbing, to say the least, yet what I found even more unsettling was his steel resolve. His eyes looked empty, hollow, but also determined on some course of action with unwavering focus.

I snuck back into the tower that night, and I wish I had not. Upon entering the dark lower floor, my senses were attacked by a virulent stench of rot which almost made me retch. A wet cloth on my face lessened the effect somewhat, and after I had lit a candle my nerves calmed enough for me to proceed to the spell chamber on the top floor. The sickening odour intensified and wafted down the stone stairs in palpable, nauseating waves, making it impossible to proceed while breathing. I took in a huge gulp of wretched air and I ascended hastily. The sight revealed through the keyhole of that sealed door froze the very blood in my veins.

My master stood in front of a ritual circle more complex than any before seen, slightly bowing to the nightmarish shape therein. Illuminated by the two large copper braziers which erupted with scarlet billowing smoke in frequent intervals, the entity stood proud over the bent humanoid figure hunched before it. It had the head of a black goat with massive horns and sharp merciless teeth, while instead of hands it possessed dark crustacean pincers. Its lower body was neither male nor female, yet it looked human, if humans were the size of oxen.

The Grand Magus spoke, yet the words of that guttural foul tongue that he used are lost in time. Despite my having studied a few languages by then, my efforts to discern some words or at least the language's roots proved fruitless, for it seemed to possess no rhyme, nor reason. Whether the creature replied is unclear because my breath ran short, and forced me to leave in a hurry. I returned to the village, but no sleep came to me that night, as an awful feeling of impending doom stalked my dreams.

The day after, my master informed me that he would be working on another spell, a much more complex one that would require a lot of preparation. He tasked me to find certain reagents that would be used in the working, many of which I had not heard of before despite my considerable knowledge of the natural world. Most of them I could purchase nearby, while for the others I would have to travel over land and in two instances over water. My teacher gave me eleven months to find all that he needed and return to the tower. Despite my hesitance, I did as I was told, although now I wish I had taken my own life instead, rather than help him with what happened next.

When I returned to the tower after my travels, I had seen a lot and learned even more, yet it all paled in comparison to what my wise adopted father had already taught me. Part of me was curious to see what his next spell would entail, and I curse myself for that foolishness. For when he realized that I had gathered everything he asked, he gave me one more task. He handed me a pouch of gold and commanded me to find and purchase a newborn babe from the nearby farmers. His instructions were to bring the child to him post-haste, under the cover of night.

I would have denied him there and then, if not for the menace in his gaze and a pleading so deep that it hurt my soul. The thought gnawed at me, whether it pained Alathaun to ask this of me, as his humanity was still present, even if bedraggled. I remembered my oath all those years ago, and I promised to return with what he asked. I had chosen to bury my heart beneath my servitude and allegiance to this once-great man.

A babe was easily found in a nearby village. The parents, struggling with six more young ones were more than happy to give me their newborn son, and accepted payment in gold along with my false promises of the child's safety. I lied, for I could sense the ill intent of my master even though I could not comprehend it. When

I handed the babe over to him, Alathaun shed a single tear and thanked me, before he sent me off to the village once more.

This time I knew better than to go prowling in the tower, as I felt that whatever foul beast the Grand Magus would conjure was not meant for mortal eyes, nor were their dealings. The next day my teacher spoke with me only through his bolted door. He confirmed the success of his second spell and instructed me with a new list of reagents for recovery, which would be required in the casting of his third and final spell. I was to return before Midsummer with everything he asked, which was still far away.

My hunger for knowledge and my damned curiosity led me to follow his instructions to the letter and return even sooner than expected, something which the Grand Magus was not very pleased about. I still had not seen him since we had parted so many months ago, but it seemed that his voice coming through the locked chamber sounded more vigorous, more youthful. I was amazed to be told that I would be assisting him in this final working to come.

With my curiosity piqued, the days until Midsummer seemed like centuries. If only I had listened to the primal instinct encircling my intestines and making my heart race on that fateful day, I might have suffered a plain death. Yet I chose to uphold my oath and comply with the Grand Magus's orders.

We met on Midsummer day in the spell chamber. To my astonishment, he looked many years younger, younger even than me. He cared not to explain how or why, but he made it a point to explain that once I had helped him with this task, as much gold as I wanted from the coffers would be mine and I would become an independent Magus. My amazement at the news blinded me to the hidden truth behind those words.

When the braziers with the reagents fumed their foul smoke into the chamber, my adopted father, my teacher, my master, came up behind me and slit my throat with a black-hilted dagger. As I lay there bleeding on the alien symbols carved on the floor, my last living memory is that of his face as he gazed at me in sorrow and shed a second tear. What happened next is a mystery, for my recollection becomes muddled for a time.

When my sight returned, I was already damned to this awful state. Neither living nor dead, yet sentient and incorporeal. My frantic search for my slayer proved pointless, as he was nowhere to be found. Alathaun's belongings, his leather-bound books, his thin pipe, and even his treasured black grimoire stood untouched in his study. I quickly discovered that I was not confined within the walls of the tower and could roam freely. Soaring through the air, a strong tingling sensation drove me toward the small pond nearby.

The stars sparkled above the sleeping village, with only a young lad there. He was crouched naked on the shore, and he gazed at the moon's reflection on the still surface of the water. The youth was no more than ten winters old, but in my altered state, I could sense that he was the Grand Magus Alathaun. I approached and tried to speak with him, but my fleshless lips could not fashion words that are normally heard. He seemed oblivious to my presence, while a look of sheer joy and awe was spread on his features. It was the pleasure from the magnificent beauty of nature first-gazed upon with the eyes of the 'ignorant'. That made me realise what my master had accomplished with his third spell. It was a spell for him to forget – everything. Who knows of the horrors he discovered in that accursed grimoire that pushed him to this decision, the same horrors that ultimately deprived him of his second chance at life.

The lad approached the pond and bent over to drink some of the murky water, when a part of the shore collapsed, and threw him into the water. Amid gurgling sounds and splashing hands, my master born anew shed his third and final tear, drowned and was damned into oblivion.

Only I still linger around the pond forevermore, and sometimes I speak of my doomed master to those who would listen. Those few special ones who cannot only hear my words but also discern the true meaning behind them. Yet I guess my mind may not be the most trustworthy of allies after all these years. This is the first time someone has stayed to hear my entire tale, and perhaps that is the way to my own absolution.

For that, I thank you.

END

UNFINISHED BUSINESS

Death comes easier every time you go through it. I should know, I speak from experience. My only hope is that the blessed dark earth covering my current tomb will finally grant me peace – this time around. My statement might seem bewildering to any logical person, but everything will become clear in this reckoning of my life and deaths.

My name is Lazarus[17] Ptolemy Fin, and I first died before I was even born. The umbilical cord in my mother's womb tried to murder me by twirling around my neck, suffocating me, as if it knew my terrible fate and was trying to spare me from it. Yet my survival instincts proved stronger, as the kicking that commenced alarmed my mother, and gave my parents ample time to get to the hospital. The doctors said it was a miracle that the resuscitation worked, because my heart had stopped for a full minute. That is why my parents, although of Egyptian descent, decided to name me Lazarus instead of just Ptolemy. They claimed that I was destined for great things. My father was an expert on Egyptian antiquities and history and thus the name Ptolemy was selected, but after my first death and resurrection, my mother insisted on taking on the name Lazarus also, a testament of her Coptic[18] faith.

I grew up in Alexandria of Egypt, where most of my carefree childhood memories were formed. My father's position as the Counsellor for the National Department of Antiquities enabled us to have a very comfortable life. Our ample family means allowed me to be home-tutored by some of the best in the country. It was on the day after my tenth birthday that we decided to move to the US, following my 'accident'.

I was playing in the garden of our estate near the fountain with the griffon statue adorning our yard, during a hot summer day that parched skin and tongue. I was pretending to sword-fight with some of my mother's more tolerant plants when a stubby snake hissed and jumped at me, bit my calf and then vanished into the shrubs. I remember the burning, numbing sensation spreading throughout my limbs before I burst into screams. Everyone rushed to my aid and luckily enough one of the gardeners, Kaddish[19], God bless his soul, managed to kill the snake. This helped the doctors identify the poison and give me the antidote after they had resuscitated me back to life, as my heart had stopped for almost two minutes.

The staff mentioned that it was a miracle I had survived with no ill effects from the extended lack of oxygen, and my parents made sure to remind me to include my thanks in my bedtime prayers.

After the incident, my mother insisted that we move somewhere safer, and pressured my father to find work in another country. My father's expertise in his field secured him a position as a consultant for the Smithsonian Institute in the US, and so we were uprooted. Hoisted into a new world, completely different from what I was used to until then, it felt like a dream. My English was broken at best, forcing me to work twice as hard to catch up in school. I kept my head down, studied hard, and even managed to find some friends during my school years, including my best friend, Brendan Holler.

I met Brendan as I was getting off school, during my first few weeks in the US. On my way to the bus stop, four kids approached me from behind and pushed me to the ground. Suspecting a mugging, I instinctively curled up into a ball and tried to protect my head from any more attacks, but none came. A burly kid with a bob cut who was their leader stepped closer and towered over me.

"Give me your lunch money, pipsqueak, and you get to go home in one piece," said the boy with clear menace in his tone.

My English was not good enough yet, but I got the gist of what he was trying to convey. They wanted my money, but I had already spent it at the school cafeteria and only had enough to buy the bus ticket home.

"No money, sorry, not one piece. One piece for to take bus home," I tried to explain in panic, taking out my bus fare change.

The act seemed to infuriate the nasty adolescent even further. He slapped my hand hard and scattered the coins from my palm. He then stepped on my chest with his dirty sneakers and pinned me to the ground.

"Then you go home in your socks," he nodded to the rest gleefully.

The other two stepped closer with giggles and grabbed my legs, while the third boy started prying off my shoes. I tried to struggle but, with zero athletic ability against four older kids, I stood no chance. Panic gripping me, thoughts of what a horrible place my parents had brought me to streamed into my mind as I heard a voice somewhere close to the scuffle that made everyone pause.

"Hey, Matthews! Harassing the new kid, are we?"

A tall blond boy in a bomber jacket had stopped with his sticker-covered bike a few steps away, and was looking my overweight oppressor in the eye. He was handsome and fearless. He made his question sound like a threat.

"Just teaching him how the food chain works, Holler, mind your own damn business," spat the despicable boy.

My blond saviour then sprung up and took hold of the air pump that was attached to his bike, while throwing the bike itself to the ground with force. The explosion of motion with the crush of the bike on the sidewalk made the group of adolescent delinquents take a step back.

"You are four against one and that makes it my damn business, Matthews. Leave... him... alone," he said and tapped the metal bike pump on his open palm as he waited for a response. In my childish eyes, he seemed radiant and daring like a superhero.

The motley group of kids looked at each other with uncertainty and took a few more steps back. As their burly leader realised what was going on, he raised his fist toward my rescuer and gave him the finger. They all started to walk away after that in haste. I was still on the ground, dumbfounded.

As I lay there shocked, a helping hand pulled me out of my trance. "Hey buddy, let me help you up. Are you OK?"

I checked my body. There were only a couple of scrapes on my elbows and forearms. I stood up with his help and nodded my thanks.

"Not much of a talker, are you? Well, as long as you are OK," the boy said and picked up his bike.

He moved to leave and I struggled to find the correct words, "I am Lazarus Ptolemy Fin. I come from Alexandria, Egypt. Nice to meet you."

The boy turned to me and smiled. "He speaks! Well, would you look at that! It's nice to meet you, Fin. I'm Holler, Brandon Holler."

He offered me his hand and I shook it in both of mine vigorously. "Thank you, Brandon Holler," I managed to say, "come my home, play games?"

My new friend smiled gently but declined to join me that day, mentioning that he had chores to do. We did meet the following day though, and the day after that, and every day since. In any case, from that point onward I remember seeing the US differently, as a place I could begin to actually enjoy living in.

My relationship with Brandon, the first person my age who didn't judge me or see me as the 'foreign kid', enabled me to break free from the turtle shell I had been hiding in until then. Despite our vast differences, we complemented each other's weaknesses. Where Brandon was big and muscular, I was slim and agile. Likewise, where Brandon excelled at every athletic activity, I did very well in science classes and math. We always helped each other out during finals. Last but not least, Brandon was a natural lady-killer, contrasting with my timid and reluctant failed attempts at finding a date. He would give me tips on how to approach the girls I liked, who where usually way out of my league, and he would encourage me to try despite the odds not being in my favour. We hung out at every chance we got between classes or chores, and my English soon improved, as did my confidence in myself.

Time passed, and when we reached senior year I had already established myself as the valedictorian of my class, accepted with a full scholarship at MIT in the field of computer programming. Brandon, who had graduated a year before me, was on a football scholarship from Florida State. Despite the distance, we managed to see each other on holidays to catch up, and party hard. It was at one of those crazy, unhinged college parties that I met Stacy, the love of my life.

She was smoking in the kitchen along with her girlfriends when I came in to get drinks for Brandon and me. My eyes fell on her and time froze. With her long dark hair, lithe figure, and the face of an angel, she looked like the girls we saw on magazine covers. Her piercing blue eyes fell on mine, and she smiled. I could not move, speak, or breathe, while my heart started doing jumping jacks double-time. I did not know how to respond. I managed to pull my eyes off her and poured a couple of drinks before almost running back to Brandon. By the time I reached him, cold sweat ran down my spine and I felt weak in the knees.

"Hey bud, thanks for the drink!" he started to say as he took the cup from my shaking hand. "Wait a minute, you look like you've seen a ghost, what's wrong?"

He guided me outside to sit on a bench where we could talk away from the mayhem of the loud speakers. He gave me some time to catch my breath and explain, while he looked at me with a concerned expression.

After a while, I managed to speak. "Dude, I think I'm in love."

Brandon's face lit up and a smirk spread on his lips. "Man, you got me worried there for a sec!" He burst out laughing and tapped me on the back playfully. "There, there, buddy, how about you show me this pretty girl and let me handle it for you? I guarantee I can get her to at least sit with us."

I gulped as I felt the earth disappear beneath my feet. "No, man, I couldn't... I could never. Why don't you go for it instead and I will just—" I managed to say before Brandon cut me off.

"Stop." He kneeled in front of me and firmly grasped my shoulders. He looked me straight in the eye. "Now listen here, Lazarus Ptolemy Fin. You are a great guy, an awesome friend, super smart, and with a great future ahead of you. Not to mention you have a great tan."

I smiled, some of the pressure relieved.

Brandon smiled back at me and pressed on. "Any girl that cannot see your real worth is not worth it. Now man up and show me this wonder girl, I'll handle the rest."

True enough, not five minutes passed while we went inside and Brandon brought her over, along with a couple of her friends. All of them giggled, clearly enchanted by my handsome friend.

The dark-haired angel smiled, offered her hand and introduced herself. My brain didn't even register her friends' names. Electrical current spread through my nervous system with her every word, or gesture. My eyes could not move away from that magnificent sight, not even for a moment. Despite my efforts to enchant her like Brandon, I failed miserably. The end of the night was a complete blur, as out of stress I had drank too much and ended up sick. Brandon did not let up though and he called me the next day.

"Hey Fin, guess what! I got us a date with Tina Johnson and a few of her friends on Friday, including *your* Stacy."

My head was still spinning from the hangover as I tried to make sense of what he had just said. "Are you for real, or are you pulling my leg?"

"Of course for real, dummy, would I joke around with something like that?"

"How the hell did you manage that?" I asked in turn.

"Well, I had to employ some of my Brandon magic, but it's done! We're meeting them on Friday at the roller park, and then for drinks later."

The splitting headache that had harassed me up to that point became a mild nuisance, diminished by the waves of excitement which coursed through me at the news.

"Well, drinks are on me then!" I screamed into the phone speaker.

Friday could not come sooner. Nighttime at the roller park meant loud music, roller dancing, and the thing I dreaded most, lots of touching. Stacy was there with her friends, and she looked amazing. Her unparalleled beauty once again left me breathless, a silent passive observer, rather than potential dating material. Stacy was staring at Brandon in scorn while he flirted with her friend, Tina. She did not spare a single glance my way, despite Brandon's brags about my academic accomplishments as he tried to 'sell me' to the girls. At some point when Tina went to the bathroom, Stacy grabbed Brandon's arm and took him aside. They stood too far away for me to listen to their conversation, but from their body language, she appeared very frustrated with him. She waved her arms and stomped her foot, as if berating him. Brandon on the other hand seemed apologetic and even pointed at me, or in my general direction. Their conversation ended abruptly when Tina came back from the bathroom, leaving me to wonder what it was about.

Soon after that, we all left the roller park and went to Tina's home for drinks as her parents were away for the weekend. On the way there I asked Brandon what was up with Stacy, but he just waved my concerns away.

"She just warned me not to disrespect Tina. Girl stuff, man, don't worry about it."

I knew my friend so I gave him a frown.

"If by disrespecting Tina she meant you'll sleep with her and then dump her, I guess she was right to feel concerned about her friend. I mean, I would do the same for you!"

Brandon laughed. "I guess she was!"

My response was a thin, uncomfortable smile.

"I think there will be some other guys at Tina's house. You just focus on getting Stacy tonight, Fin. Something tells me your chances are looking good."

"Really?" I asked incredulously.

"Really, bud. By the way, I call parents' bedroom!"

I almost jumped with joy.

When we reached Tina's home, the after-party was well underway. There were a dozen people there already including Stacy, all well into their drinks. As soon as we sat down, Brandon started making out with Tina. Stacy's glare spat brimstone and lightning at them. It was only after Tina had taken Brandon by the hand and led him upstairs that she turned to me.

"So, Lazarus, was it?" she asked in a mild slur, well into her third drink already.

I offered a smile, trying to hide my surprise that she remembered my name. Most girls did not.

"Yeah, but my friends call me Fin. You're Stacy Callaghan, we met at the house party last week. I was with Brandon when—"

"You are Brandon's friend, right? The one he keeps talking about how smart he is and how successful he will be after college?"

The unexpected compliment made me flinch like a physical blow.

"I... guess?" I managed to mutter.

She drained her plastic cup and slammed it on the table. She then turned and gazed at me with her brilliant pools of blue ice.

"Are you good friends with Brandon, Fin?"

I laughed and fixed my hair.

"Yes. We are best friends. To be honest, if it weren't for Brandon—"

Her thin, delicate finger on my lips stopped me abruptly. She bent closer and whispered in my ear, "Do you want to make out, Fin?"

She smelled like alcohol and cigarettes, mixed with a sweet scent of vanilla. I could not speak, so I just nodded. It was then that Stacy Callaghan, an angel from heaven sent to earth just for me, kissed me.

The college years passed in a flash, with Stacy and Brandon by my side. I lived in constant bliss, with a woman that I worshipped, and a friend whom I treasured. Stacy was initially against Brandon and his behaviour towards women. She said that he was a sexist and a player, not to be trusted around women. Fortunately, after heavy prompting and convincing by me, she agreed to give him a chance. After college, I managed to get a job at a small computer company, which after a few short years became an international sensation. As the company's success was mainly attributed to my innovations in integrated algorithms for computer systems, they offered me the position of CEO.

With my high-end salary, Stacy and I got married and moved to a beautiful house with a white picket fence in the suburbs. We could easily afford a private backyard, private garage, large TV and all the modern commodities. Brandon of course became my best man. We were living the American dream. Brandon visited at every chance he got between games or when he was in town, and never failed to share his extravagant stories with us. He played as a quarterback for the Washington Commanders and his scores were great for a few years, but his athletic accomplishments did not last very long. He was forced to quit after a serious knee injury during one of his games. Following the end of his football career, my dearest friend immersed himself in an ocean of alcohol and meaningless relationships, which made my heart ache. After several attempts, I managed to convince him to join an A.A. group and move into our house for a while, at least until he got his feet back under him.

Seeing my dear friend in that sorry state, I decided to create a company of my own that would specialize in what I did best, computer algorithms. I hired Brandon in a middle management position, and helped him get a house of his own close by. The company was a hit, and soon enough it soared into the top 20 most successful companies in the US. Money was no longer an issue for me, so I focused on trying to create a family with Stacy. Alas, it was not meant to be, as after we visited specialists we found out that we could never have children the normal way with my sperm count. The doctors offered us the option for *in vitro* fertilisation, but Stacy continued to refuse, no matter how hard I tried to convince her otherwise.

Slowly but steadily, she grew reclusive and distant. She winced at my touch, and pulled away at any display of affection on my part. Even though she never complained about the absence of children in the house, the sorrow in her eyes was evident every time we met couples who were blessed with offspring. Meanwhile, Brandon visited for dinner every so often, providing me with valuable advice on the intricacies of the female psyche, despite his already two failed marriages. Stacy would become more conversational and attentive following his visits, but that would never last more than a week.

I began my efforts to rekindle our passion by buying her extravagantly expensive gifts and taking her on exciting trips around the world, something she had always dreamt of. It was on one of those trips which we made to my native Alexandria in Egypt that everything changed.

It was summer and the relentless sun burned even hotter than I remembered from my early childhood. We had not visited Alexandria since we moved to the US with my parents all those years ago, and everything looked new to me, but also strangely familiar. We had just settled into our five-star hotel and taken a leisurely stroll around the colourful marketplace when my eyes fell on the glass window of a small shop. The sign read HEBA'S TRADITIONAL EGYPTIAN JEWELLERY, and even though the cheap stuff that was on display did not deserve a second glance, the aged woman who waved at me to come over certainly did.

She was very old, with creased, wrinkled skin on her aged face and hands. She wore a colourful shawl that fell on her bony shoulders, and her neck was adorned with several necklaces of varying lengths. My approach was hesitant, but her dark eyes and her toothless smile completely disarmed me. She spoke in Egyptian and her voice resembled a warm, musical carpet.

"Hello, sir, peace be with you. Could I interest you in a very special gift from my shop?"

I smiled awkwardly.

"Peace be with you. That won't be necessary, I think my wife has already had her fill of gifts for today, we are on our way to our hotel."

The kind, warm expression on the ancient woman's features changed to that of concern. She leaned in closer.

"This gift is for you, not for your wife." She waved her bony finger left and right for emphasis, before she continued.

"It is a very special ancient jewel, blessed by the Gods to bring good fortune to those who wear it. Why don't you come inside and have a look, before you decline my offer?"

The woman's demeanour puzzled me. Her tone sounded more like a challenge than an attempt to convince me to purchase something from her shop. Intrigued, I offered a polite smile and entered. She ushered me inside and, after she closed the door behind me, she turned the little 'closed' sign to face outward. That made things even weirder, but my curiosity made me stay. The aged woman slowly began to walk behind the register and gave me another of her toothless smiles.

"I am Mama Heba[20], welcome to my shop!"

The old lady bent behind the counter and I heard a drawer slide open. She then took out a small box made from polished wood, adorned with an ankh[21] symbol on its beautiful lid. When she opened the ornate box, I saw that a jewel made of gold, and some sort of precious dark-green stone lay within, carved in the likeness of a scarab beetle. I recognized the representation from my father's photos and books of famous Egyptian symbols.

"That's a scarab amulet, thought to bring about good luck, and it relates to the sun-god, Ra, is it not?"

The woman's dark eyes glimmered with satisfaction.

"That is correct, my son. More specifically, this is a heart scarab[22] amulet and it is a symbol of rebirth and transformation. It carries all the knowledge one requires to answer the questions of judgment correctly, and ensure one's place in the afterlife when Maat weighs their heart. It is extremely old, blessed by priests of Ra in old Egypt. Look here, it contains the proper spell inscribed on the back, straight from the Book of the Dead[23]..."

At the sound of that I tensed a bit, but the old woman turned the amulet over and passed it to me to examine. The amulet was indeed a thing of beauty. The beetle figure was carved with excruciating detail on the dark, rich green stone, almost lifelike. Banded with gold leaf, it was set in place on a gold base, and on the back I could see tiny hieroglyphs painstakingly carved. A thin gold wire was in place at the top, to enable a person to wear it around their neck. From my experience with artefacts my father would occasionally bring home, I could tell that the beautiful jewel was ancient and not some sort of cheap copy for tourists.

"This is beautiful, but I am not sure how 'legal' it is for me to purchase this from you," I said, in an effort to politely decline. This thing should be worth a fortune.

The woman smiled her toothless grin.

"I am the legal owner of this artefact and I have all the necessary paperwork from the Department of Antiquities. If you are willing to purchase it, there is always a way to send it to you wherever you may go. As for Mama Heba and her credibility, feel free to ask around."

The relic of a woman paused and allowed me to consider it for a few moments. Seeing my reluctance, she added, "You look like you can afford it, and I can assure you that you will need it. I would not offer it otherwise, as it has been in my family for many generations."

I gazed into her dark eyes questioningly.

"What do you mean that I will need it? I'm not dying."

Her expression changed into a grim disposition tinged with sorrow.

"From the moment I laid eyes on you, I saw a dark shadow hanging over your shoulders. That is the shadow of death. I'm sorry that it fell on me to tell you this, my son."

Somehow, I could feel the sincerity of her words. My neck hairs stood on end.

"I'll take it. How much do you want for it?"

Her reply came swift and steady. "Ten thousand dollars, US," she smiled.

When I exited the shop, the weight of the ornate amulet felt reassuring around my neck, and cool where it touched my chest under my shirt. Stacy waited for me nearby and looked as exasperated as ever.

"What took you so long? What was that old woman trying to sell you?"

Several cigarette butts lay stomped on the ground around her. A nasty habit she had taken up again a few years ago, despite knowing about my displeasure at the smell.

"Life insurance, I guess," I said jokingly. Stacy did not find it funny.

When we returned to the US, my relationship with Stacy started to improve a bit due to Brandon's frequent dinner visits. Meanwhile, I followed all the instructions Mama Heba had given me and never took the scarab amulet off, even while I slept or bathed.

Despite the old woman's words of reassurance, my company looked her up and it appeared that she was well-known and respected in Alexandria, for helping others with her practices of magic for more than 40 years. An examination of the amulet by an expert jeweller was also conducted, and he informed me that it was made from serpentinite and pure gold, well worth the cost. Soon enough things started to look up as an offer for my company, which came to a few billion dollars, was made by a competitor.

When the news reached Brandon and Stacy during one of our dinners, they were both amazed. When I saw their excited approval of going forward with the buyout, I decided to do so. My only non-negotiable term for the agreement was that Brandon would get to keep his position at the company after the buyout. As for Stacy and I, we would finally have all the time and money in the world to do whatever we wanted. She even told me she would consider us adopting a child or two, and that made my heart sing. After the buyout deal was successfully completed, Stacy offered to cook a very special dinner to celebrate the future. Alas, that would be the last dinner the three of us would ever have together.

The wild boar was cooked to perfection that night, and Stacy even gave me a few naughty looks full of promise before dinner. We were all dressed in our finest. We enjoyed the delicious food and wine, and we discussed what we would do with all that money and made jokes. Everything was perfect. The dining area in our home was neatly decorated with festive balloons and congratulations posters. The moon shone brightly through the glass-framed door that led to the garden, and the beautiful willow trees that swayed gently in the evening breeze. When my glass of extravagantly expensive wine had emptied, as I reached out to refill my plate with some of that glorious meat, I felt a stab of pain in my chest. My left arm numbed and my breath faltered, and I barely managed to stand up and croak Stacy's name as she gazed at me in alarm. I tried to reach her with an outstretched hand, to touch that angel of otherworldly beauty for one last time, when the floor rushed up to meet me. Through my hazed eyes, Stacy crouched over me and Brandon made a call. I could hear he was talking to 911. In response, Stacy burst into tears while Brandon embraced her gently with his free hand. Darkness enveloped me.

I opened my eyes but could not see anything. All that could be heard was silence. I tried to move but there was not enough space. The realisation of being confined in a wooden box dawned on me in horror. I was in a coffin! An instinctive scream left my mouth while I struggled, but instead of my normal voice, I heard a deep, incoherent growl, more bestial than human. The sound made me pause for a bit. I wondered if I was dead then, but, since I could move, hear, and see, I reckoned I had escaped death once again, only to be buried alive. I started to pound my hands and feet on the lid and the sides of my prison with renewed vigour. The stout, hardened oak wood of my coffin gave way under my blows as if it were made from cardboard. Cold, wet earth rushed in to cover me along with bits of splintered wood. Slimy maggots writhed across my skin and in my mouth. My hands reached into the moisture-filled soil and frantically pulled me upward. Slowly but steadily, I ascended. One foot after another followed and pushed me upward. My hands finally broke the surface of that muddy embrace, bringing me to freedom.

It was night and raining hard. The full moon was hiding between dark clouds, its halo barely visible. Reflexively, I took in several big gulps of air after the strain, until I realised I did not need to.

Am I dead, or alive? I wondered.

As if in answer to my unspoken question, the weight of the heart scarab suddenly felt revitalizing on my chest. It was warm, burning almost. I looked around and realised that this was the same cemetery my parents were buried in, as per my last will. I moved to the graveyard's entrance only to find my way was blocked by the heavy gate which was locked shut. Desperation and frustration made me grab at the bars and pull them apart with all of my strength. I half-expected to hear my shoulders or wrists pop, but the thick iron bars instead strained and bent like aluminium straws beneath my grasp. After a few moments to orientate, only a single thought burned through my mind: to see Stacy.

Out of habit, I checked my gold wristwatch. It was very late and it poured. Catching a ride this late would be impossible and, as it was expected, they buried me without my cell phone. The cemetery was only a few miles away from our home. All that was needed now was to walk through a small forested area before I could reach my destination. It would not be long before I got to hold her in my arms again. As I came closer, a tug in my guts led me onward as if my life, or stranger still, my very soul depended on it. I hastened my step.

The house was lit up like a Christmas tree despite the lateness of the hour. To my surprise, the backyard entrance was open. Dirty and wet, my footsteps light, I proceeded through the willow-filled garden to get a glimpse inside the house without giving my beautiful wife the scare of her life. I peaked through the large, glass door that overlooked the garden, and there she was. Mesmerizing as always, with a high-cut, elegant red dress that complimented her curves, and her long raven hair a silken cascade that ran down her lithe back, she was speaking on the phone. Her face was flustered and her eyes shone with excitement. Against my every urge to knock on the glass door to get her attention, the scarab amulet flared in protestation, making me hesitate. I leaned in closer to listen instead.

"Are you almost here, baby?"

She paused and listened.

"Alright then! I left the backyard gate unlocked for you. Remember to park a couple of houses away now. OK, see you soon, love you too!"

She hung up the phone and went to the hallway mirror to fix her hair. I jumped to the side so as not to be seen by the reflection. The grassy earth beneath me felt like quicksand and a bottomless pit rapidly grew in my stomach. Thoughts and possible scenarios raced through my mind, as my subconscious tried to make up excuses to explain what I had just heard. Yet it was clear enough what had been going on.

A large shrub next to the window served as my hiding place. I waited patiently to see what would happen. That gut-wrenching feeling of the world collapsing was only verified when I saw Brandon, good old best friend, best man, Brandon, as he strolled casually through the garden. He looked sharp as always. With a bundle of red roses in one hand and an umbrella in the other, he moved to the front door and gently knocked. As I still stood there, I slowly emerged from my hiding place to see Stacy hug and kiss him passionately, flowers and umbrella abandoned on the white-marble floor. His strong hands clawed hungrily at her slender back. I stood there and watched until they finally stopped. Stacy took Brandon by the hand and led him to the dining area. I stood outside under the pouring rain, and anger began to boil up inside me.

Brandon spoke first. "So, everything went as planned after all. I can't tell you how happy you have made me, my love, not to mention rich!"

They both giggled.

"I know, baby, but do you think it was easy for me? Remember, I was the one that had to sleep with him every single day, and live in the same house!"

Brandon's handsome face brightened, and he gave her another fierce kiss. After a couple of passionate moments that felt like centuries to me, he placed his hands on her shoulders and kept her at bay.

"Of course, I know how much you have sacrificed these past few years. Do you think it was easy for me to see you in his scrawny, geeky arms? All I want is you, and I don't even care about the money or anything else. That's why I did what you asked me and poisoned my 'best friend'."

She beamed.

"About that, are you sure the poison will not be discovered?" she asked with a tinge of fear in her eyes.

"Yes, I'm sure. Since it did not come up in the morgue's report, unless a specific toxicology analysis or an autopsy is requested by his next of kin, who in this case it is you, by the way, they will never find out. We are home free!"

"We are also filthy rich!" she shouted and sprung into his arms again.

The frothing, bubbling anger swept through my innards like a tidal wave, and turned everything into a blood-red haze. I burst through the glass door straight into the dining area. Broken shards flew in all directions from the force of my stride. Startled, they both crashed onto the floor still embracing each other. Their wild eyes were open wide in terror, as they realized whom they were facing. Stacy screamed. I took a few steps toward them and tried to ask Brandon why he had betrayed me this way. Instead of words, a deep growl emanated from deep within my throat. Stacy screamed again, and this time fainted into blissful unconsciousness. Brandon sprang up and stepped back with caution as he raised his hands in defence.

"Now wait up, Fin, this is not what it looks like. I can explain if you just give me the chance. You are my best friend, you know that! I would never betray you! Right, bud?”

Seeing his uncertain smile made me remember all the times he had stood by me, helping me, defending me, and even rescuing me. My old friend's squeaking voice and words of reassurance made my anger multiply tenfold, and my pain and sorrow likewise. My charge came with a roar, while my dirt-covered fingers searched for his muscular neck. As I stepped in, he bashed me on the head with a vase from the stand next to him, but I felt nothing. He tried to punch me with a growl of his own then, only to have his arm broken like a twig as my arms flailed about. He tried to scream for help just as my hands closed in on his throat. I squeezed my unmoving hold slowly, firmly, until I heard a satisfying *pop*. My friend's eyes filled with blood and plopped to the marble. His limp body crumpled to the ground and I stepped on his head, again, and again, until there was nothing there but a red blotch on the white marble floor. I took my attention off him and looked around. Stacy was still unconscious. She did not look beautiful any more.

I went to my office and grabbed a pen and paper to write down these words:

Apparently, my third death was not the last, but this time I know it will be. I will now go back to where I was buried and finally pass over to the afterlife. As for my lovely angel of a wife, I will bring her along for the ride and allow her to explain when our hearts are judged on the Scales of Maat. Unfortunately, without a scarab of her own. You will find us there, in our final embrace. Death will not do us part.[24]

END

BLOODY

I was born more than three millennia ago, yet I still do not know the reason for my existence. It is true, life everlasting has been granted to me, albeit in the shadows. They say it is not good to start a story with a contradiction, but alas, here I am already doing it thrice. I have come to accept that it is a fault of my character, to try that which few would, and do what others should not. I do not deem it a burden, as it has enabled me to become who, or what, I am. I have seen empires crumble and others rise in the passing of the centuries, the same as I have witnessed people and their stories become contorted by belief or prejudice, transmogrified into something else entirely. In my experience, time possesses that transformative power over the collective human consciousness. That's how legends are born.

After having lived for so long, I have decided on an endeavour that is opposed to my nature and my warrior spirit. One might wonder why I have not put the story of my life in ink until now, but a grim tale such as mine is not something easily spat. You will have to forgive my manner, as I am unskilled in using the pen. My skills lie elsewhere. They lie in the fiery spirit of battle against a worthy opponent, wielding naked steel to bring about swift death in the night. In fighting tooth and claw to overcome the enemy, in gaining victory at all costs. I am a hunter that hunts those who hunt. My name is Caelan[25], son of Njord[26] the Berserker[27].

My father was a Norse Gael[28]. His father, Ulf[29], had come from the North already a renowned Berserker Warrior, in search of greener pastures. He settled in the green land of the Celts and proved his skill in battle many a time. In honour of his skill, he was allowed to marry one of the locals, the fire-haired Deidre[30]. She gave birth to my father, Njord. My father grew up to be strong and fierce, and eventually became a great warrior in service to the young king Tigernmas[31]. The king valued my father's skill and rewarded him with the hand of the raven-haired Caoimhe[32], who descended from the line of Laignech Fáelad[33], the first of the wolf warriors. It was so that my blood came to possess not one but two dark gifts, that of the burning red rage, and the heart of a wolf. Two dark gifts, that made me who I am today.

My fearlessness and ferocity were well noted from a very young age, in the constant competition with my four siblings over everything. We would fight regularly and minor injuries would often occur, but my blows would never harm them seriously. In time, they learned to be cautious around me and to respect my strength. No more than seven winters old, in a red haze of fury I cracked the skull of our neighbour's oldest boy with a rock, after he had insulted one of my sisters. The 12-year-old did not die outright but was instead mortally wounded and lay on the brink of death for many days. When he could finally walk and talk again, he stumbled to our doorstep to apologize and asked for my sister's hand when they came of age, as a means to reconcile our families. To my amazement then, my father looked at me with a great deal of admiration and allowed me to decide. After asking for my sister's consent, who already liked the boy, I accepted his apology and gave them my blessing. My chest swelled with pride.

The story of my first victory was spread through the mouths of all children in the surrounding area, and provided me with the beginnings of the fame that later turned to legend. Our household was a warrior's home, so we all grew up trained to fight with muscle and bone, but also with weapons.

Danger was ever-present in those times, be it marauding warriors or wild beasts, so the need to defend oneself was vital for survival. Bloodshed was not a strange sight to our youthful eyes. I still remember the first time I held a real sword in my hand, a gift from my father. Although heavy for my adolescent muscles, it did not feel like a foreign body to me. That beautiful bronze blade was an extension of my arm, an extension of myself. I marvelled at how it sliced through the air, slaying my imaginary foes. My heart raced as if my blood was aflame.

It was then that I knew I was born to wield the sword, or so I thought. For my fate held a darker, grimmer turn.

After my 13 winters and in all aspects considered an adult by that era's standards, the dreams started. I saw myself run through a darkened forest under a moonlit sky, chase down my prey and sink my teeth into it. The thrill of the hunt, to run wild and free for miles, and the thrill of the kill, forced me to awake doused in sweat night after night. At the time, I considered it a side-effect of the burning red rage I had inherited from my father's legacy, yet when I asked him about it he had no answer. To my surprise, my mother explained everything during one of our mushroom-gathering ventures into the forest. Her words ring true even still like it was yesterday.

It was early spring and the forest was alive with the calls of songbirds and the smell of wildflowers. Her long silken hair shone with the light of the reflected sun, as she paused and gazed at me with her deep, dark eyes, a basket full of mushrooms in one hand. Her voice was tempered steel, and her usual soft demeanour had vanished.

"Hear me, son, and hear me well. You were told when you were a child that my blood is of Laignech Fáelad, and so my offspring carry the same blood also. That means you, Caelan, as well as your siblings, have the potential to become true wolf warriors. I have watched over all of you for signs of Laignech Fáelad blood, but your siblings have not shown any. On the other hand, you have. You see, it starts with the dreams."

I stood stunned in my ignorance and did not know how to reply to that statement. I opened my mouth to ask how and why, only to be cut off before I uttered a word.

"Take care, child. I only said you have the *potential* to become Laignech Fáelad. For us to find out, you will have to be tested."

This time I remained silent despite the blood that rushed through my veins, and waited to hear more.

"When the summer is nearly over, you will travel to the plains of Magh Slécht[34] to the West and join the wolf warriors in worship of the God of the Mound, Crom Cruach[35]. It is there his golden figure stands, surrounded by twelve others, and it is there you shall be tested. If the God of the Mound deems you worthy, only then can you become a true Laignech Fáelad. Until that time comes, you should prepare. You must speak of this to no one, not even your father."

My throat was dry from the suspense, for all these words were only mentioned in stories around the fireplace, or in ceremonies that honoured the gods. I swallowed hard and managed to utter one question:

"How will you know if the God of the Mound chooses me, Mother?"

Her smile was simple and sad, and so was her reply.

"I will know if you return to me alive, for it can only mean that you were chosen."

Only then did I realize the gravity of her words that day.

Summer could not end soon enough. After I had learned about the test of Crom Cruach, all my following days were spent honing my skill in axe, sword, and spear, and made my strikes truly sharp. Chasing after goats, rabbits, and deer in the forest until my feet bled granted me the swiftness and agility of a predator. Pushing heavy logs against the current of a nearby river steeled my muscles. Whenever I was not training, I either slept or ate. My father was initially against my overwhelming determination to obtain strength at all costs, but after a very long private discussion with my mother, he objected no more. As a result, my rigorous training had sculpted my body as well as my will, into a weapon.

By the time summer was ending, I had grown half a head taller and could lift the sword my father had gifted me with. It was then that my mother told me to make ready and travel to the plains of Magh Slécht to meet the wolf warriors. My father would accompany me up to a point close by, but would not come any further as the gathering was exclusively for worshippers of Crom Cruach. Njord the Berserker worshipped no God, but respected my mother's wishes.

We rode for three days across meadows and creeks, tree-filled glades and open plains before we reached the plains of Magh Slécht. When we arrived, we stood in silence for a while and gazed at the figures that gathered in the distance. Thin tendrils of smoke rose in the clear sky from several campfires, and lazily swayed to the rhythmic pounding drums. My heart began to gallop and I tensed when I felt my father's gaze upon me.

"We are here. This is where the worshippers of the old God of the Mound gather in worship. I did as I promised your mother, out of respect for her beliefs. You know that I worship no God, other than the strength of my limbs and the reach of my sword, but I also want you to know this: You are my son and you carry my blood as well. That alone will enable you to become a great warrior. If you choose to follow and worship Crom Cruach, it does not mean that you have to abandon the red rage that is your legacy. As for me, I will not think less of you if you do so. After all, the king I serve, Tigernmas, also worships that same God. You have already proved to be a worthy son."

I tried to speak but I felt my voice about to crack, so I chose silence. I squared my jaw, gazed into my father's deep blue eyes, and nodded grievously. The giant bear of a man lifted me with one arm from the saddle and placed me on the ground gently. He then offered me a fierce smile and slapped his horse's rump. The magnificent steed whinnied and galloped the way we had come. I stood and watched until he disappeared from my sight before I allowed my burning tears any release. They tasted of pride and sorrow. After I had swallowed the last of my tears, I walked steadily toward the gathering ahead, the weight of my bronze sword reassuring on my thigh.

I was greeted with the angry stares of wild men and women, stark naked other than the wolf skins they wore as cloaks. Tiny huts constructed from sticks and tanned leather were strewn around a circle of twelve stones. In the middle of the circle lay a golden figure with a single eye in the centre of its forehead, and its arms spread wide. Its teeth-filled mouth was open, ready to devour its offerings. In its open palms, the figure held grain and milk.

A few of the wolf-cloaked men surrounded me then, sniffed me like beasts and issued menacing growls. My hand instinctively went to my bronze sword and I could feel that the red haze had started to bubble forth in my stomach. I managed to stifle it and I introduced myself by stating my intention to become a wolf warrior. The men laughed at my words and explained that, since I had come here willingly, I had already offered myself as a sacrifice to the God of the Mound. If I survived the test, only then would I be granted a place among them and spared the blade. As soon as they had my consent, they howled in unison and even more people surrounded me. My instincts told me to run but my determination was stronger, as muscular, sinuous arms unclothed me and threw away my possessions, including my sword. They gave me a white garment to wear and ushered me to a pen where other younglings had been herded. There were no more than 12 boys and girls of varying ages there. All of them wore the same white garment as me. One of the girls had a babe in her arms and cradled it gently. A couple of the younglings were around my age but all the rest were older. At some point, we were given milk and bread to eat. There we waited until the sun slept, to be sacrificed to the God of the Mound or to be chosen as one of the wolf warriors.

Night fell as the beating drums intensified. The moon rose over the plain and covered everything in its pale glow. Some of the gathered followers danced around fires, howled at the moon, and offered milk and grain to the golden figure in the middle of the stone circle. Young animals were slain, and their blood was used to draw symbols on chests, arms, and faces. I could feel my heartbeat align with the hypnotising drums, and I could smell incense and herbs that were being burned to fill the air. The campfires, which blazed brightly now, added their fiery sheen to the light of the moon and made shadows come alive around us. I began to fall into a trance-like state. When the silver disc was high in the sky, a brutish man opened the pen door and guided us to the stone circle in a line. All the worshippers stood in anticipation, as we were instructed to proceed into the circle one by one and then to touch the golden figure in the middle. Next to the God of the Mound stood a wise old druid[36], who wore the skin of a white wolf and wielded a large knife in one hand, with his wrinkled skin covered in tattoos of blue paint. The first youngling entered the circle, a boy not many winters older than me, and reverently placed a hand on the God's mouth. The old druid then asked Crom Cruach to accept their offering, sharp dagger raised high above his head. Everyone stood silent for a few breaths, while the drums pounded in unison.

A red sinister brilliance pulsed from the God's eye, and at the same instant a thick, billowing mist began to spew forth from the base of the statue. The druid's knife fell on the young boy's neck, and splattered blood onto the golden figure. The worshippers howled in unison, like a blood-crazed wolf pack. The same happened over and over again until many bodies of younglings lay on the bloodstained valley floor in front of the God of the Mound. When my turn came, memories of everything my father and my mother had taught me flooded my mind, and made me remember who I was. I took a deep breath and placed my palm on the bloody mouth of the golden idol, waiting for the knife to strike. The crimson light of the eye of the God of the Mound lessened upon my touch, and focused into a narrow beam that illuminated the centre of my chest.

The wise druid lowered his blade and loudly announced for everyone to hear, "On this night we have another member joining our pack, Caelan, son of Bjorn."

In my trance, I did not realise what had happened, until my white garment was taken away and the pelt of a young grey wolf was tied around my shoulders. Everyone howled, and I howled with them. Other than me, only one more youngling was selected to become Laignech Fáelad, while all the rest were put to the blade as an offering to Crom Cruach, including the innocent and defenceless babe. That left a bitter taste in my mouth and a stain on my warrior's spirit. I now understood why my father did not worship this cruel God. Yet my choice had been made, and there was no turning back. I was a member of the pack.

Before I returned home, I spent a few days with the other Laignech Fáelad. Their training taught me how to use numbers against a single enemy, how to distract my foe to allow my brethren to attack from the rear, and how to expose my enemies' weaknesses to ensure their demise. Those techniques first encountered during those few days changed my perception of battle, and placed savage reasoning on the gift of rage I had inherited. I began to envision the initial inklings of how the two could be combined. After I had completed the training, it was made clear to me that strength comes with the pack, and by working together rather than fighting alone in a blind haze of fury.

Despite the knowledge that had been granted to me, I returned home with obvious discontent. Several days were spent in arguments with my father about the honour of slaying a babe who was innocent and utterly helpless, but all of his responses gave me no satisfaction. Njord the Berserker would never betray the oath that had been given to his King, an oath of blood that bound him forevermore.

Asking my mother for guidance granted me no reprieve either, as she was a stout believer in the Old Ways. I still remember the day when I confronted her. She hung wet clothes to dry and softly hummed a lullaby. She had her dark hair bound tight up high, and her white skin glistened with sweat from the shimmering sun. As if the crisp northern breeze notified her of my intent, she hung the last of my father's goatskin chemises and turned to me, in anticipation of the question she knew was coming.

"Mother, did you know that this God of the Mound demands the sacrifice of younglings to provide succour from illness and to grant bountiful crops?"

Her gaze did not shift from her bedraggled determination.

"Of course I know, my son. Those of my bloodline have worshipped Crom Cruach from times immemorial, since the beginning of our line, with Laignech Fáelad. It is a sacrifice of the few, for the prosperity of the many."

I was astounded at her lack of empathy and her brisk manner. I could not believe that my own mother would tolerate the sacrifice of defenceless young souls to a grim, merciless God such as this one. Yet it was not my place at the time to oppose her, nor the path she had shown me.

I kept training and meeting with the other Laignech Fáelad every full moon. The meeting places were never the same but it would always be members of the pack only.

No others were allowed. After I had spent some more time with them, a slight relief came when I learned that the cruel God required the sacrifice of an infant only once every year. This somehow lessened my dissatisfaction with this practice, but the foul, bitter taste that stained my mouth every year during the Crom Cruach festival still remained. My summers grew grim in anticipation of the bloodstained celebration, so I chose to focus on my training to numb my feelings of disapproval.

The years passed and I grew stronger, mightier. I had fought in many battles as a member of the pack and had proved my skill every single time. When 20 winters were behind me, none could best me among the Laignech Fáe-lad. Some of the elders took offence at my pride and I prevailed on several challenges for duels to the death. Great warriors all, yet none could withstand my berserker fury combined with the lethal tactics of the pack. This only aided in expanding my fame further, as more than a score of them had fallen to my blade over the next five winters. My name made ripples in the world.

It was during that time that King Tigernmas, a middle-aged man by then, came to visit the Laignech Fáelad and ask for their aid in battle. I was there when he offered copper, silver, and gold for our services, and was declined on all accounts. My wolf brethren hungered for blood. The elders asked the king to sacrifice his next offspring as soon as it was born to the God of the Mound. The king immediately agreed, and the pact was sealed. When I saw them grinning at each other, it sickened me. The red rage came over me. Visions of blood and mayhem filled my eyes and prompted me to slay everyone there and then in that goatskin tent. Fortunately for me, my time with the Laignech Fáelad helped stay my hand that night, as it would have been suicide. I decided to bide my time and take my revenge on that heartless king, that cruel God, and my accursed brethren alike when the opportunity presented itself.

I did not have to wait long.

A short while after my change of heart I was hunting deer in the forest. I had tracked the beast in complete silence, and stalked it until it came to a stop to drink some water from a shallow stream. I notched an arrow and aimed for a killing blow as I held my breath. In the instant before I took the shot, a wolf like no other I had ever seen stepped into view.

Its massive head stood well over my belly, and I was considered a tall man. Its thick paws conveyed strength with every step. The fur around its expressive amber eyes and elegantly taut ears was dark brown. On its sniffing snout were blotches of a lighter shade of the same colour, while its cheeks and proud neck were powdered white. Muscles bulged on its powerful front and hind legs, and its puffy tail was lowered. It was without a doubt larger than any other wolf I had ever seen, but what struck me as odd were its eyes. Those slanted amber orbs, with flecks of gold dancing in their depths, spoke of an intellect far superior than any simple beast should possess.

My surprise almost made me loose the arrow and I barely managed to hold the wolf at bay. It looked straight into my eyes, as if it expected something from me, or judged me. During my time with the Laignech Fáelad, we had often heard wolves sing with us at night, but none had ever approached us this close. Puzzled, I lowered my bow with frustration since my hunt had just been ruined. To kill a wolf for no reason or to steal a wolf's prey was prohibited among the Laignech Fáelad.

"Get out of here, you damned wolf, or I shall slay you and keep your pelt to warm me in the winter. The only reason I do not kill you straight away is because you are spirit brother of the Laignech Fáelad."

The wolf paused and did not move. It only gazed at me with those large, intelligent eyes. When it opened its mouth, instead of a growl came a deep voice that was rich with experience. I could feel it reverberate through the soil into the soles of my booted feet, while through the air it filled the rest of my body. I shivered.

"You speak of the wolf warriors as if you are one of them, boy. Tell me then, what do the Laignech Fáelad stand for, what do they believe in?"

To hear a wolf speak in a man's voice caught me off guard and I paused. Those were dark times indeed, where many a strange beast or malevolent spirit could be found to roam. I had heard tales of the origin of our order around the campfires, of a man said to be able to take on the form of a wolf. With my curiosity piqued, I continued the conversation.

"They are the wolf brethren. Descendants of Laignech Fáelad himself, the man who was a wolf and the wolf who was a man. They are all great warriors and they worship Crom Cruach, the God of the Mound. What of it, creature?"

The enormous predator shifted its weight and drew a thin smile on its black lips.

"You speak of the pack as if you are not one of them. Why is that, Caelan?"

I took a step back and drew my sword, my bow and arrow forgotten on the ground. I gritted my teeth and I felt the hairs on the back of my neck stand up, as the hot rage bubbled forth from my gut.

"How do you know my name, creature? Speak, or I will end you."

Feeling my killer's intent, the wolf tensed and growled but did not attack. Weary of my every movement, it replied, its deep voice tinged with menace. "You dare bare your fangs at me, pup? I know a great deal about you, Caelan son of Njord, for I have watched you and I already know the answer to my question. I have watched you howl at the moon with the rest of the pack, I have watched you slay a number of them who dared challenge your strength, and I have watched you gain victory alongside them under the banner of a mortal king. Most importantly though, I have seen you bite your lip and clench your fists when your brethren bear the sacrifice of the newly born to this God of the Mound they now worship. I know what is in your heart, I have smelled it. You worship not this cruel God and find your brethren's practices despicable. That is why I chose to speak with you; for you carry my blood, child, and it appears you also have my heart."

I stood speechless and wondered if this wolf who spoke in a man's voice before me was actually Laignech Fáelad, or some foul sorcery. My heart was beating fast in anticipation of battle, but the red rage slowly faded away. My instincts told me it spoke truthfully. I lowered and sheathed my weapon, ablaze with curiosity to know more.

"If you are indeed my ancestor and we share the same blood, then tell me the whole truth, please."

My reply seemed to appease the deadly beast and it relaxed, and the gold-flecked pools that were its eyes pierced right through me.

"Very well. Hear me then, my descendant, and I will let you decide the truth of my words, and that of your heart. Our line goes back to times immemorial. It is as old as the world itself. We are warriors, yes, but we do not fight for others, we do not fight for gold, we do not fight for glory, and we definitely do not fight in honour of a demon from the Old World, like Crom Cruach. We fight to protect this world and its people and keep at bay the things that hunt men like cattle. We are protectors, first and foremost, of the weak and defenceless. Since the beginning, those of our bloodline could shift like me into the shape of a wolf. Our fur could not be easily cut or pierced by conventional weapons. We numbered by the thousands spread across the land, and only came together when needed.

"We took part in the Great War alongside chieftain Érimón[37] against the Tuatha Dé Danann and their magic tricks. The war was fierce and lasted for years. It took a great toll on us, as the enchanted blades of the Immortals cut through our thick hides like butter. Our numbers were greatly diminished, and by the time we managed to drive the Tuatha Dé Danann[38] from this world, only a few scores of us remained. The Immortals understood that without the strength of our bloodline, they would have prevailed against the humans. They used the services of a demon of the earth from the Old World to kill and enslave our kind, the one you know as Crom Cruach. Chained by the magic of the Immortals for millennia, it was unleashed upon the mortal world once again with one purpose only: to eradicate and corrupt the Laignech Fáelad. As long as it succeeded in this task, it could feast freely upon the blood of the living as it desired. The demon used foul magic, lies, and poison by night to kill every one of our blood who refused to worship him, except me. Those who chose to worship him lost the wolf's gifts forever and were forced to offer their firstborn offspring as a sacrifice to what was then called the God of the Mound. It took that name from the mound of corpses laid before it. To ensure its victory, the vile entity ingeniously demanded the blood of the newlyborn to be sacrificed in its name. As long as Crom Cruach's hunger for blood was satiated, bountiful crops and healthy livestock would be granted to its worshippers."

The wolf's eyes grew saddened, and it paused. It gazed outward for a few moments as if it relived the past, before it continued.

"The revenge of the Tuatha Dé Danann did not end there. They cursed me with life everlasting so I could continue to produce offspring, yet none of my blood would any longer possess the ability to shift into the form of a wolf. Until that is, someone who has both my blood and my heart would appear. That someone is you, Caelan, son of Njord. I have waited for a very long time for your arrival. You will become the instrument of our bloodline's revival.

"I charge you to find those amongst your pack that share our hearts and make ready to shed blood. The blood of all those who fight for the demon God Crom Cruach, including the rest of your brethren. The time for the battle will come sooner than you expect. Starvation, sickness, and death will descend upon the land. People will ask for help from the Gods, as they always do. It is then that you must strike at Crom Cruach and disrupt the sacrifices to starve him out. But be wary of its corrupting magic. The demon can transmit its hunger for blood to the living and the dead, I have seen it happen many a time in the past. Once proud warriors, turned into blood-sucking monsters of the night, neither living nor dead. When you have managed to starve out the God of the Mound, its magic will be greatly diminished and this will release us from its curse. The true Laignech Fáelad will be restored."

My fear was gone, obliterated by the words I had just heard. So it was true that there was something more to being a wolf warrior than just howling at the moon and sacrificing babies to a cruel God. I felt a deep satisfaction in knowing that my heart was in the right place. I knelt then for the first and last time in my life, in front of the great beast that was my ancestor.

"By the clouds in the sky, by the waters of the rivers, by the earth beneath my feet, and by the fire of lightning, I will fight to restore our blood to its proper path. I will be the instrument of our revenge against Crom Cruach, the God of the Mound. I will slay my brethren if I have to, and everyone else who stands in my way. All this, I swear."

The beautiful, strong predator's eyes never left mine as I spoke my oath. After I had finished, it nodded once and then moved away until it vanished into the shrubs.

Now that I was left alone under the shade of the trees, my determination crystallised and my mind filled with visions of revenge.

The wolf's words came true soon enough. The crops failed and the animals got sick. Sick were the people too, from a burning fever that lasted for a week. Most would survive it, but too many perished that winter. Shadow spread upon the land. The people feared and discontent grew. It is said that the aged king Tigernmas visited the Druids, and several seers on what to do, but everyone had a different opinion. Some claim the king had been over-come by old age and fear, and so he decreed that every family in his kingdom that had newborn babies would sacrifice them in the name of Crom Cruach.

That royal decree raised many objections and the peo-ple grew outright angry, as not all of them shared the same beliefs. I grasped my chance then, and gathered those of my brethren who would listen to reason and join me against this injustice. No more than a score gathered, all of them sword brothers and sisters, great warriors of the pack that knew honour. To convince them to fight along-side me was easy enough, as the newborns in the whole kingdom numbered in the hundreds. A sacrifice such as this was unheard of. It was genocide. After long discus-sions, it was decided that I would lead the attack which would take place during the ceremony on the last month of summer. In the meantime, my true wolf brethren and I would search for more warriors to join us in secret.

We remained in touch and exchanged information by using our full moon gatherings with the rest of the Laignech Fáelad. News of the sacrifice spread like wildfire and we were able to find many who were willing to fight alongside us. Each of us had a score of warriors behind us by the time summer neared its end. On the night before the sacrifice, we had gathered 400 strong near the plains of Magh Slécht, and had laid out our plans. From the in-formation we had gathered, King Tigernmas would have his entire army along with the rest of the Laignech Fáe-lad on his side, which meant that we were outnumbered five to one. Thousands of people would also gather at the location, those forced to sacrifice their babies along with those who willingly gave them up. We believed that if the ceremony was disrupted and a battle broke out, the people who were forced might join us and tip the scales in our favour. It was so decided to disrupt the ceremony on four sides and draw out sections of the king's army into the surrounding groves. A select few of us, including myself, would then rush through the openings in the lines and kill the king as well as the druids conducting the sacrifice.

On the eve of battle, there were no inspiring speeches or words of encouragement. Only a shared, grim determination of men and women brave enough to stand against injustice and protect the people. Some prayed, others sharpened their blades in silent contemplation, while a few drank wine and ate bread. We scattered by first light and took positions, in anticipation of the gathered crowd which we knew was on the move from our scouts.

First came droves of people all dressed in white. Many of them cradled babes in their arms under the sound of drums. To our surprise, even greater numbers than anticipated had come to the plains of Magh Slécht. We were uncertain whether most of them were worshippers or not, but our doubts faded when we saw tears in the eyes of many of them. The number of infants being carried to the location was staggering. As for the cries of the babes, they were almost drowned by the lamentations of the adults. People suffered around the golden figure of that Demon that stood surrounded by its 12 dark stones. A druid stood in front of each stone and one more druid was next to the golden idol. A fire rose in all of us hidden in the woods then. It burned so bright it was almost visible in the twilight. The druids soon moved with the setting sun, and provided honeyed wine to silence the crying babes as well as soothe the ailing parents. As the last rays pierced through the gloom, they fell upon the shining armour and glistening weapons of King Tigernmas's army. To the sides of the army walked men and women who wore nothing but wolf pelts, with their weapons sheathed. Our once wolf pack, doomed to die by our hands on that night. Fortunately for me, my father had perished with honour in battle a few years ago and I would not have to face him also.

The moon rose high and the sound of the drums intensified. Everyone took their positions and the king struck a pose of reverence. He foolishly remained in the front of his army near the standing stones. Lines of infants carried by their parents dressed in white, spread like pale vines amidst the dark crowd, as they waited for the ceremony to begin. When the gathered Druids began to chant, everyone fell silent. The rhythmic beating continued, and a thick, heavy fog began to gush forth from Crom Cruach's idol. A reddish glow filled the night, bathing it in blood. This was our sign. I drew my trusted sword and felt the night breeze beckon me to battle. My blood boiled as the burning rage rose from my guts and filled me up to the brim. With a low growl, I signalled the others to attack. We ran in silence to cover as much distance as possible, before we burst into howls of fury and battle shouts that instantly broke the droning of the gathered crowd.

My first kill was a blonde man no older than 20 winters who prayed in reverence to the God of the Mound. His hand was on a small axe ready to pull it out, when my blade sliced through his neck. His head toppled to the ground with an expression of surprise frozen forever on its features. Three more worshippers fell before another one came at me with screams to his god's name, a large axe raised above his head that aimed to cleave mine off. The tall, burly man swung hard but missed me entirely as I tumbled behind him and sliced at his calves. He fell in agony, with blood gushing from his severed legs at each dying breath. My rage built up and threatened to take away all reason. I barely managed to keep it at bay while I sliced, punched, and chopped left and right. I tried to carve a bloody way to the king. The trail of death behind me made many of the gathered reconsider attacking me, and most in proximity dropped their weapons and ran, while others took heart and fought alongside us. Everything progressed according to plan.

Bodies fell as we pressed on through the gathered crowd until we finally reached the regiment of soldiers that guarded King Tigernmas. They maintained a tight defensive formation and created a wall of heavy copper shields that glistened in the firelight as if ablaze. Veteran warriors all, with grim expressions and weapons at the ready. I knew then that we stood no chance against such an organised and well-equipped opponent. I paused for a few short breaths and my mind spun to find some reason to hope. I found none, and so I abandoned reason. I allowed the burning red fury of my berserker heritage to come over me, fill every fibre of my being, and consume me entirely with its blazing fire.

My battle howl sounded across the battlefield and made the king's soldiers pale with fear as I ran towards them and crashed on shining shields like a storm front wave on a small fishing boat. Their line broke and I revelled in their despair. I sliced through hands still gripping their weapons and feet that tried to run away to my right, disembowelled bellies and chopped off heads to my left. No blade, no armour, no shield, could withstand the fury of my blows. In my blinding haze, I barely noticed the king who hid behind several of his cronies and started to move toward him. His fear stank as he cowered under that crimson light and billowing mist. Behind the king, the druids screamed to Crom Cruach. They begged for forgiveness and pleaded for aid.

I could barely hold my sword from the slippery blood that covered the hilt, so I punched the next man straight onto the nose guard of his copper helmet. Blood spattered and the metal bent beneath my blow, along with the man's face. I threw my sword into the neck of the woman behind him and watched her die gurgling blood as I picked up the dead man's sword. The few remaining soldiers around the king took a step back as if they sensed their doom, while the king himself screamed at them to stand their ground. Behind the tightly knit group, the druids still pleaded with the merciless God. This time their prayers were answered, but not as they would have wished, perhaps.

The dense mist obscuring the battlefield pulsed and moved with a life of its own. Its colour took on a deep red hue as if it absorbed the crimson radiance that spewed forth from Crom Cruach's golden idol. The blood-tinged mist swirled around the bodies of the fallen and entered through their open mouths, eyes, ears, and nostrils. The mists also surrounded the druids, who screamed in agony, and it sounded like the air was being sucked out of their lungs. The freshly slain bodies twitched and moved, as their eyes filled with blood and their skin turned deathly pale. Before my very eyes, I saw their teeth grow into sharp fangs and their nails into vicious talons. The creatures attacked everyone and used unimaginable strength and blinding speed to deadly effect. They fell on the living like locusts on fresh grain and sucked their blood with their sharp teeth. People screamed in agony as they perished.

The creatures seemed to not be affected by mortal blows, something I soon discovered when I disembowelled a woman-turned-monster whom I had just sliced through the throat moments ago. She kept coming at me and screamed for blood, with her intestines sprawled at her feet and her throat in gory tatters. The creature only stopped when a strike of my sword severed its head clean off. In a mayhem of blood spatters and red mist, the druids slowly rose with eyes like red-hot coals that shone eerily. Bat-like wings sprouted from their backs and their skin had turned black and leathery. Their teeth resembled serrated knives and their talons short, curved swords.

As I turned to face them, a voice like none I had ever heard before blasted through the field. It was deep and gurgling, guttural, and spoke in a strange tongue. Its resonance and depth were such that everyone, including me, fell screaming to the ground. I gritted my teeth and mustered my rage to come forth. In my mind, I saw my father usher me forward to trust in my heritage, my mother to place me in the hands of a demon god out of ignorance and fear, the friends and allies I had lost, the defenceless babies.

What happened next, I cannot accurately explain. My heart felt ready to jump out of my chest. Wave after wave of purifying, all-encompassing rage came over me, total and absolute, but there was also something else there. The beating heart of a wolf. I rose then, changed into an instrument of death. I could see, smell, and hear more. Every scent had a name and a meaning. I could smell blood everywhere, and on the bloodsucking creatures, I could also smell death. I could hear the heartbeat of people around me apart from those that turned into monsters, I could hear their screams of death. Thick, dark fur had grown all over my body and every injury I had thus far sustained was completely healed. Immense strength and potent vigour coursed through my body and I abandoned my weapon. I did not need it any longer.

The transformed druids shot through the air with blinding speed toward me, and slashed at me with their sword-like talons, all the while screeching horribly. The first one that did so was easily evaded with my newfound otherworldly reflexes. The second one that came right after, I grabbed hold of its ankle as it flew past, whirled it once, and used the momentum to slam it hard into the ground. With a wet crunch, the creature splattered blood and remained motionless, broken. Two more flying demons rushed at me and landed on my back. They used their ruthless talons to pierce through my chest and slice my neck. I managed to protect my throat and I had suffered only a deep gash on my back before I grabbed hold of both of their necks, and ripped off their heads. More came, and more fell, until only a couple of the transformed druids remained. They screeched in anger but did not continue fighting. They chose to vanish into the night sky instead.

My gaze turned to the golden idol and the surrounding stones. The red light was greatly diminished, and had almost flickered into nonexistence. As I felt the Demon's strength ebb away, I approached the stone circle and picked up a large hammer from one of the fallen soldiers. The surrounding dark stones gazed judgingly full of bitterness and hatred but could do nothing to halt my advance. In my new, all-powerful form, I stood in front of the golden idol of the God of the Mound and raised the hammer up high, with the intent to destroy the statue with a single devastating blow. In that instant, the voice that had come from deep within the earth sounded again in my ears, and threw me to the ground with convulsions of pain. This time though, I could understand the words.

"You have exacted your revenge and my curse on your bloodline is no more. I will leave this place, Caelan, son of Njord, but I will not forget you. You will be cursed with life everlasting like your predecessor, only to see me eat the world and drink its blood through my servants. You may have won this fight in your minuscule mortal mind, yet you are far from winning the war."

The crimson brilliance vanished, and the red mists which had gathered throughout the plains evaporated. The field was strewn with dead soldiers, the druids were dead or vanished into the night, and the king's head lay on the ground with the crown still upon its brow.

We had won.

My shape returned to normal after the battle, and left me sore from the many wounds I had suffered. I joined my brethren who were still standing, no more than a dozen blood-covered men and women. The 13 of us on that day took a sacred oath: to continue our fight against the darkness and to protect the people with our lives. We would bear offspring and guide them to the proper way of Laignech Fáelad. The war with Crom Cruach and its bloodsucking monsters would carry on until one side was victorious.

Millennia have passed since that night, but I still remember it as if it were yesterday. A moment when people rose against supernatural evil and corrupt authority to fight injustice. Now I fight for those who cannot in the shadow of night, where my prey hunts its own. In my long life, I have slain more of these bloodthirsty servants of Crom Cruach than I care to count, vampires they are called in the modern world, and other terrors of the night scarier still. Yet, I will continue to do so as long as I draw breath. My resolve will not falter in the bottomless of eternity. For I am the red fury of Laignech Fáelad, Caelan, son of Njord.

END

APPENDIX

<u>Diary of a Flesh Eater</u>

1. The expression 'the ramblings of a madman' is a tribute to H.P. Lovecraft, and his character Abdul Alhazred, the crazed Arab who discovered the Necronomicon while lost in the desert.

2. *Fazul* translates into 'choice', while *Hazem* translates into 'strong-minded'.

3. Constantinople, otherwise known as Istanbul, fell to the Ottoman Empire in 1453 A.C.

4. In the Babylonian myth of creation, Enuma Elish, the South Wind, assists the god Marduk in trapping the monstrous Tiamat.

5. The Hafsids were a Sunni Muslim dynasty of Berber descent who ruled Ifriqiya (modern-day Tunisia, western Libya, and eastern Algeria) from 1229 to 1574.

6. Hyenas have been loosely associated with ghouls, and there are some who claim that ghouls can shape-shift into the form of a hyena. Some Arab cultures believe that striped hyenas are grave robbers, while others claim that

a striped hyena can put a spell on people before dragging them to their lair to devour them.

7. The name is a tribute to 'One Thousand and One Nights', one of the earliest appearances of ghouls in literature. Specifically, it comes from night 624–680, where Ajib and Gharib come across Sa'dan the Ghul and his five sons.

8. *Hadith* is the Arabic word for a 'report' or an 'account' of an event. In this case, it refers to what the mainstream schools of Islamic thought believe to be a record of the words, actions, and the silent approval of the Islamic prophet Muhammad, as transmitted through chains of narrators. Legend has it that certain Hadiths could be used to convert a ghoul to Islam and to convince them to abandon their evil ways.

9. According to folklore, ghouls can be driven away or killed by prayer, or by a single strike with a sword. If the ghoul receives two or more strikes, it will return to torture and devour its assailant.

10. Jannah is the final abode of the righteous, or paradise. Jahannam is the place of punishment for unbelievers and evildoers in the afterlife, or hell.

11. Another tribute to H.P. Lovecraft, who describes ghouls as living underground, or roaming in abandoned subway stations, feasting on victims of train wrecks.

12. Midsummer is a celebration of summer. Usually held at a date around the summer solstice, it has pagan pre-Christian roots in Europe. According to folklore, Midsummer Eve was thought of as one of the spirit nights of the year, where the veil between the material and the spirit world grew thinner.

13. Magic, according to folklore and occult philosophy, was considered the highest form of art, and therefore it was usually capitalised as Art.

14. According to folklore, blood oaths were extremely powerful and binding. Breaking such oaths was believed to bring doom and suffering to the offender.

15. Three is considered to be a magical number, and the Rule of Three is an integral part of many magical teachings. This number appears throughout the story again and again as a means of reflecting that association (three blood-drops, three spells, three tears).

16. Grimoires are magical textbooks that contain information on spells, rituals, the preparation of magical tools, and lists of ingredients and their magical correspondences.

Unfinished Business

17. The name *Lazarus* is derived from the Hebrew Eleazar, meaning 'God helped'. Lazarus of Bethany was a character in the bible, who Jesus Christ brought back to life from the dead, four days after his passing. Claudius

Ptolemy was an Alexandrian mathematician, astrono-
mer, astrologer, geographer, and music theorist.

18. The Coptic Orthodox Church, also known as the
Coptic Orthodox Patriarchate of Alexandria, is an Ori-
ental Orthodox Christian church based in Egypt, serving
Africa and the Middle East.

19. The name *Kaddish*, also found as *Qaddish* or *Qadish*,
is a hymn praising God that is usually recited during Jew-
ish prayer services.

20. The name *Heba* comes from Arabic, and translates
into 'blessing' or 'gift'.

21. The ankh, or key of life, is an ancient Egyptian hiero-
glyphic symbol used to represent the word *life*, and by
extension, as a symbol of life itself.

22. The heart scarab is an oval scarab artefact, usually
an amulet made from serpentinite, dating from ancient
Egypt.

23. The heart scarab was used in reference to Chapter 30
from *The Book of the Dead* and the weighing of the heart
being balanced by Maat, goddess of truth, justice, order,
wisdom, and cosmic balance.

24. A play on words, opposite from the 'until death do
you part' of a wedding ceremony.

<u>Bloody</u>

25. The name *Caelan* comes from Gaelic, and it translates into 'slender'.

26. The name *Njord* means 'north' in Scandinavian, and is also the name of the Norse god of the wind and sea.

27. Berserkers were great warriors, frequently mentioned in Old Norse written corpus as being able to enter a frenzied state while in combat, and fight with exceptional ferocity.

28. The Norse–Gaels were a people of mixed Gaelic and Norse ancestry and culture.

29. *Ulf* is a name common in Scandinavia and Germany. It derives from the Old Norse word for 'wolf'.

30. The name *Deidre* comes from Gaelic, and translates into 'broken-hearted' or 'sorrowful'.

31. Tigernmas, son of Follach, son of Ethriel, a descendant of Érimón, was, according to medieval Irish legend and historical traditions, an early High King of Ireland.

32. *Caoimhe* is a name of Irish origin, meaning 'beautiful'.

33. In medieval Irish, English and Norse works, werewolves were said to have been the descendants of a legendary figure named Laignech Fáelad, whose line gave rise to the kings of Ossory.

34. Magh Slécht is the name of a historic plain in Ireland. The death of the High King of Ireland, Tigernmas and 4,000 of his followers in the Seventh Plague of Ireland,

occurred there while worshipping Crom Cruach on 31 October (Samhain, Halloween), 1413 B.C. His grave is marked by a standing stone.

35. Crom Cruach was a pagan god of pre-Christian Ireland. References in a Dinsenchas poem in the 12th century to sacrifice in exchange for milk and grain suggest a function as a fertility god. On the other hand, the description of his image as a gold figure surrounded by twelve stone or bronze figures might point to a function as a solar deity.

36. A druid was a member of the high-ranking priestly class in ancient Celtic cultures. Druids were religious leaders as well as legal authorities, adjudicators, lorekeepers, medical professionals and political advisors. Druids left no written accounts.

37. Érimón, according to medieval Irish legends and historical traditions, was one of the chieftains who took part in the Milesian invasion of Ireland, which conquered the island from the Tuatha Dé Danann, and one of the first Milesian High Kings.

38. The Tuatha Dé Danann, meaning 'the folk of the goddess Danu', also known by the earlier name Tuath Dé, meaning 'tribe of the gods', are a supernatural race in Irish mythology. Many of them are thought to represent deities of pre-Christian Gaelic Ireland.

ABOUT THE AUTHOR

Christopher Balis is a Greek artist and entrepreneur, born in 1984. He has a BA in business administration and an MSc in human resource management, and has extensive working experience in the humanitarian sector. Under the pseudonym Polytropos, he has been active as an author of dark fantasy and horror stories, an RPG game writer with several acclaimed publications, and a songwriter of contemporary music and medieval fantasy music. Having lived in Greece, the UK, and Cyprus, he currently resides near Thessaloniki, with his beloved shepherd dog Lisa.

You can learn more and follow at: polytroposart.com